180 Fun and Challenging Science BrainTeasers for Kids!

SURPRISING SCIENCE

By E. John De Waard and Nancy De Wa[a]rd

GoodYearBooks

An Imprint of ScottForesman

A Division of HarperCollinsPublishers

GoodYearBooks

are available for most basic curriculum subjects plus many enrichment areas.
For more GoodYearBooks, contact your local bookseller or educational dealer.
For a complete catalog with information about other GoodYearBooks, please write:

GoodYearBooks
ScottForesman
1900 East Lake Avenue
Glenview, Illinois 60025

ISBN 0-673-36312-0
Printers Code 1 2 3 4 5 6 7 8 - SY - 03 02 01 00 99 98 97 96

Illustration: Tom James. Design: Lynne Grenier.

Insects have six legs and usually two pairs of wings. Spiders are wingless and have eight legs, and many capture food with webs. What is a winged, six-legged creature in a web?

Want to see a rainbow? Fill a jar with water and place it in a sunbeam on a windowsill. Put a piece of white paper on the floor where the sunbeam hits. What makes the rainbow?

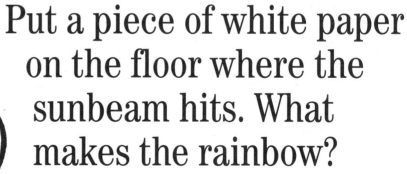

SURPRISING SCIENCE

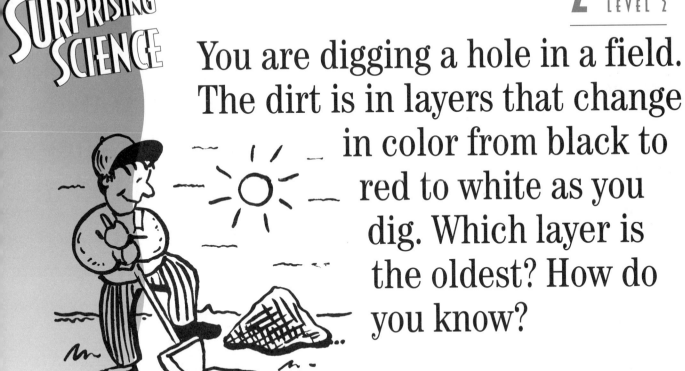

You are digging a hole in a field. The dirt is in layers that change in color from black to red to white as you dig. Which layer is the oldest? How do you know?

"CHEESE!"

Cameras are an important part of our lives. Without cameras, you couldn't take pictures. The first camera was invented in 1839. It did not use film. What did the first camera use to make pictures?

How are plants and prisons alike?

SURPRISING SCIENCE

You use energy every day for light, transportation, and warmth. Energy can be changed but not created or destroyed by ordinary means. Where does the energy go after you've used it?

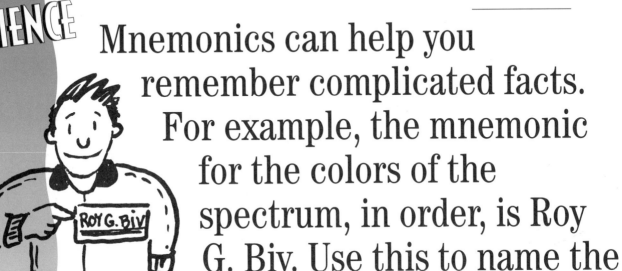

Mnemonics can help you remember complicated facts. For example, the mnemonic for the colors of the spectrum, in order, is Roy G. Biv. Use this to name the colors of the spectrum.

Mountains wear down at about 1 foot every 900 years, producing small particles that are carried away by water or wind. Often these particles pile up and turn back into rock. What kind of rock is made this way?

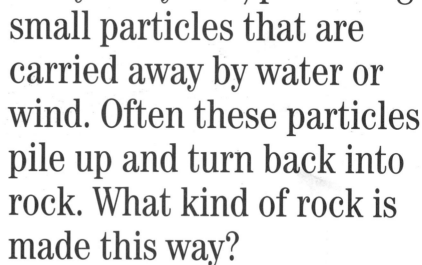

FALLING ROCKS

SURPRISING SCIENCE

The human circulatory system contains about 60,000 miles of blood vessels. If all of the body's blood vessels were placed end to end, how many times could they circle the Earth?

Last winter Nicole moved to a brand-new house. The telephone and power wires in front ran straight from pole to pole. One day in July she noticed that the wires had drooped down. Is this a problem?

SURPRISING SCIENCE

In science, words are chosen carefully to accurately describe things. For example, one small part of a meter is called a centimeter. What part of a meter is a centimeter?

When you touch something hot, it is easy to see how heat is conducted to your hand. However, most of the heat on Earth comes from the sun. How does the sun's heat get here?

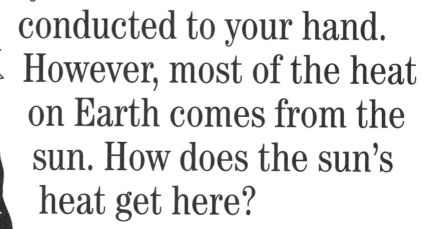

SURPRISING SCIENCE

Betty the Amazing Cat!

Living things have many things in common. They also have unique properties. What can cats do that no other animal can do?

When you breathe in, your diaphragm muscle contracts and makes your chest cavity bigger. Why does air flow in when your diaphragm contracts?

The point at which bones that move come together is called a joint. For example, your elbows have joints that act like hinges, called hinge joints. What type of joint is in your hip?

You are walking across a flat field and find a large boulder. This rock is made from material that is not present in other rocks less than fifty miles away. How did the boulder get to the field?

Carl has found a fascinating chemical compound. Using things he found in his kitchen, he was able to change it from a solid to a liquid to a gas. What is it and what makes it change?

Poof

Because you cannot see it, it is hard to believe that air has density. But it does. Which is more dense, warm air or cold air?

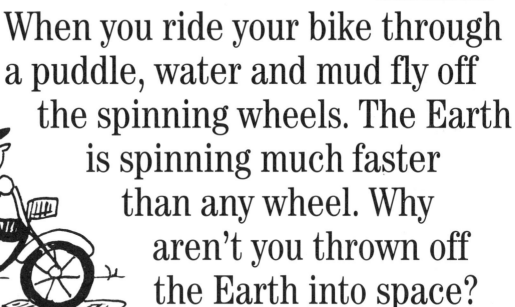

SURPRISING SCIENCE

When you ride your bike through a puddle, water and mud fly off the spinning wheels. The Earth is spinning much faster than any wheel. Why aren't you thrown off the Earth into space?

Have you ever watched cows standing in a pasture? They seem to be chewing gum! But they are really chewing a cud, a wad of tough grass fibers. Do other animals chew their cud?

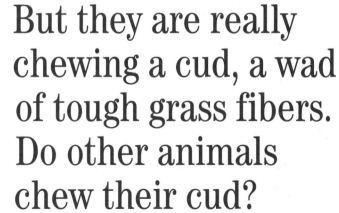

SURPRISING SCIENCE

When a volcano erupts, molten rock flows out over the surface. This type of rock is known as igneous rock. Where does igneous rock come from?

The spine is one of the most important body systems. It is made up of 26 separate bones and supported by muscles and ligaments. What makes the spine such an important part of the skeletal system?

SURPRISING SCIENCE

What do you call a 24-hour period when rabbits eat all the vegetables in your garden?

We are used to seeing many kinds of trees and flowering plants. This is because we live in a moderate climate where plants grow quickly. Do plants grow above the Arctic Circle?

ARCTIC CIRCLE 4,000 Miles

The average human has about ten pints of blood in her body. In one day the heart circulates this supply about one thousand times. How many gallons of blood does the heart pump per day?

The Grand Canyon is one of the scenic wonders of the United States. It has been forming for millions of years. Was the Grand Canyon formed by glaciers?

The metric system unit for length is the meter. It is easy to work with because it is subdivided into units that are multiples of ten. What is one-tenth of a meter called?

Did you know that water is a nutrient? You could go without food for several weeks, but you cannot go without water for more than a few days. What makes water so important?

Arteries, which have high pressure, carry blood away from the heart. Veins carry it back even though the pressure in the veins is quite low. What keeps the blood in veins going one way?

Rondell sprained his ankle. The doctor told him to soak his ankle in warm water and afterwards to apply hot towels. How is the heat traveling throughout Rondell's ankle?

All complex structures are made up of smaller parts. For example, a building can be built of concrete blocks or bricks. What is the basic unit from which all living things are made?

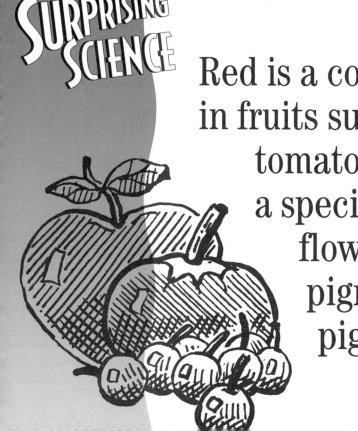

Red is a color that you often see in fruits such as apples and tomatoes. It is produced by a special pigment. Even red flowers contain this pigment. What is the pigment called?

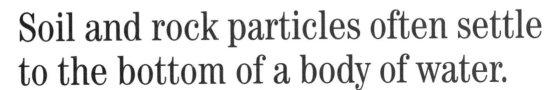

Soil and rock particles often settle to the bottom of a body of water. These deposits are called sediments. As sediments build up, the pressure turns them to rock. What are these rocks called?

Have you ever heard the expression, "blind as a bat"? Bats are not actually blind, but they do not see well. How are bats able to fly at night without bumping into things?

The mass of an object is the measure of how much matter is in that object. The mass of an object is always the same. What is the basic unit of mass in the metric system?

BONEHEAD!

Has anyone ever called you a "bone head"? You should not be upset if they do. Bones in the skull serve a very important function. It protects your brain. How many bones are in your skull?

When you walk to the store in the summer, your shoes push you along easily. In the winter, those same shoes may slip, slide, and cause you to fall. What causes the difference?

Most meteors burn up when they enter Earth's atmosphere. You may have seen them on a summer night as falling stars. Large meteors have fallen on Earth, however. How do we know that?

Living things often have many similar cells that work together in performing a task. For example, heart muscle is made of one kind of cell. What are these similar cell groups called?

the Fabulous Blood Cells working Out...

Rocks require a lot of force to break. Road builders use jack hammers and dynamite to break up rocks. But in nature, rocks are broken up by another method. What breaks up rocks naturally?

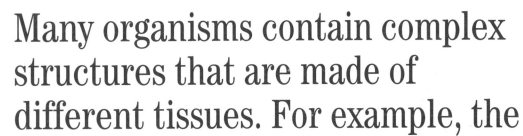

Many organisms contain complex structures that are made of different tissues. For example, the stomach consists of muscle, lining, blood vessels, and other tissues. What are these groups of tissues called?

Many people like to eat at fast food restaurants. But a hamburger and French fries every day may not be the best kind of diet. Why is this not healthy?

Some objects are harder to move than others. A brick is harder to move than a block of plastic foam the same size. The brick has more inertia. What causes inertia?

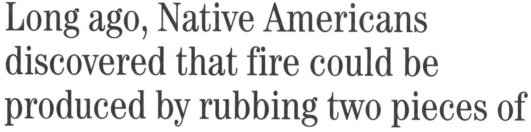

Long ago, Native Americans discovered that fire could be produced by rubbing two pieces of dry wood together. You can get a similar effect by rubbing your hands together. What produces this heat?

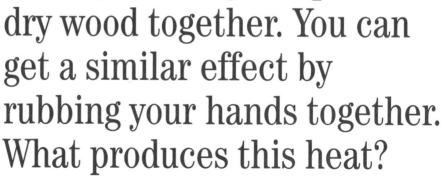

Limestone was delivered to Nancy's house to cover the driveway. She noticed that many of the rocks had split, and there were images of fish in it. What did Nancy find, and how did the image get there?

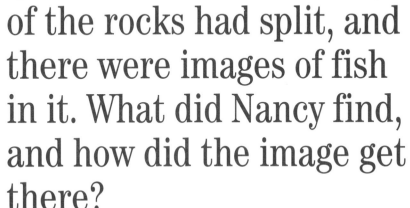

SURPRISING SCIENCE

Stacey is preparing for an important track-and-field competition. Her coach told her to eat a high carbohydrate diet. What are carbohydrates?

CARBS!

A bowling ball and a marble were dropped at the same time from the third floor of a building. Which one will hit the ground first?

Mistletoe, which is used for holiday decorations, is actually a parasite that grows and feeds on trees. It is different from most parasitic plants in one way. What is that difference?

SURPRISING SCIENCE

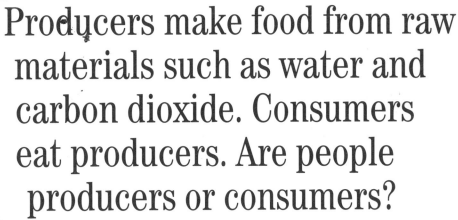

Most living things are either producers or consumers. Producers make food from raw materials such as water and carbon dioxide. Consumers eat producers. Are people producers or consumers?

Ducks spend much of their time in the water, but their feathers never seem to get wet. What is the reason ducks are able to stay dry?

SURPRISING SCIENCE

Human blood is about 55% liquid and 45% blood cells. Red blood cells carry oxygen, white blood cells fight disease, and platelets help the blood clot. What is the liquid part of blood called?

SURPRISING SCIENCE

The grasses are the most common plants in the world. The oldest cultivated plant, wheat, is a member of the grass family. How long have people been growing wheat?

Caroline was washing out plastic soda bottles before recycling them. She used hot water and put the caps back on. A short time later she noticed that all of the bottles were crushed. What happened?

In the Alps, most of the mountains over 13,000 feet have at least one glacier. In the Rocky Mountains of Colorado, there are mountains over 13,000 feet. But they do not have glaciers. Why?

THE ALPS

If you touch a hot stove, you quickly pull your hand away without thinking. This is a stimulus-response reaction. But some responses take longer. What stimulus changes some animals white in winter?

The weather near large lakes is changed by what meteorologists call "lake effect." How do large lakes affect weather?

Hawaii is surrounded by the sea. Yet, in many areas, there are no fossils found as you dig down through the rock. Why?

SURPRISING SCIENCE

Your skin helps regulate your body's temperature. How does it do this?

Newton's third law states that for every action there is an equal and opposite reaction. Blow up a balloon and let it go. Explain what happens.

Everyone has heard of the "wise old owl" but is an owl truly wise? Probably not. Crows and geese may be wiser than the owl. What is the most intelligent bird?

Most complex organisms require two parents to reproduce. However, some plants and animals can reproduce with just one parent. What is this type of reproduction called?

Animals such as squid, snails, and clams are mollusks. Most of these animals are not very large. But some giant clams are enormous! How big do some clams get to be?

SURPRISING SCIENCE

On cold days you can "see" your breath as you exhale. You actually make tiny clouds when your breath hits the cold air. What does this indicate about what you exhale?

When a football player kicks a field goal or a pitcher delivers a curve ball over the plate, one very special joint enables them to do this. What kind of a joint is it?

SURPRISING SCIENCE

Horses and camels can carry several hundred pounds. Olympic weight lifters can lift more than their own weight. Who are the weight-lifting champions among animals?

Thousands of years ago, great sheets of ice, called glaciers, covered parts of northern Europe and North America. How do we know that the glaciers were here?

Natural blonds can have up to 140,000 hairs on their head. Individual blond hairs are very thin so blonds tend to have more. What is the average number of hairs on a person's head?

1..2..3..4...

SURPRISING SCIENCE

Heat energy can be transferred between objects. When you iron, heat is transferred from the iron to the cloth. From where does the heat energy in a hot sidewalk come?

Hundreds of years ago a monk named Mendel crossbred tall pea plants with short ones. Then he planted the resulting seeds. Did Mendel's plants become tall, medium, or short?

Protein is an important part of a good diet. It is called one of the building blocks of life. How is protein important in your diet?

One of the Apollo 15 astronauts dropped a feather and a hammer from the same height on the moon. They fell to the moon's surface at his feet. Which one hit first?

Some people believe that ostriches bury their heads in the sand to escape danger. But this is not the way that these birds protect themselves. How do ostriches really escape danger?

SURPRISING SCIENCE

Some of the earliest animals that have been found as fossils had bodies that were divided into three lobes. What are these extinct animals called?

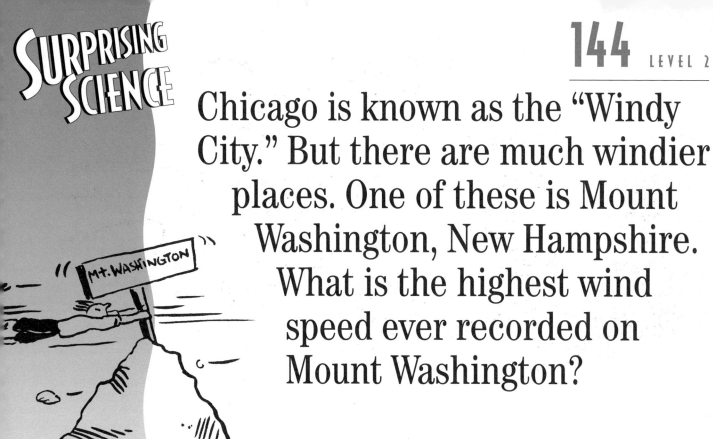

SURPRISING SCIENCE

Chicago is known as the "Windy City." But there are much windier places. One of these is Mount Washington, New Hampshire. What is the highest wind speed ever recorded on Mount Washington?

What do you call an eye specialist from southwestern Alaska?

Anthropologists can tell the sex of a person, their age to within a few years, and their health by their bones. How can bones tell so much about a person?

DANGER AHEAD

A big problem in California and other places is landslides. Hillsides erode when heavy rains occur. What held the hillsides in place and what caused them to move?

Floods take place every year in some part of the world. They do great damage because of two characteristics of flooding. What two characteristics cause most flood damage?

Take a pencil with a slip-on eraser over one end. Lay it across your finger. Can you balance the pencil across your finger? Explain how this happens.

SURPRISING SCIENCE

The temperature of an object is a measure of its kinetic energy. You nibble a warm cookie. What can you tell about the kinetic energy of the cookie versus your cold milk?

Host

Small pieces of living matter, smaller than any cell, can only reproduce by entering other cells. When they do this, they often make the host sick. What are these small pieces of living matter?

SURPRISING SCIENCE

DEFENSE SYSTEM

SKIN

One of the most important organs of your body is your skin! It is also the largest organ. How does your skin protect you?

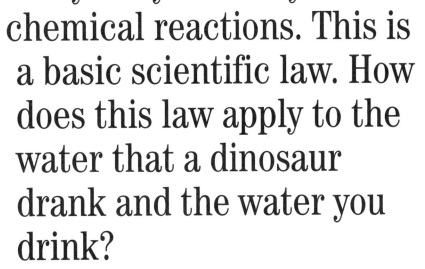

Matter cannot be created or destroyed by ordinary chemical reactions. This is a basic scientific law. How does this law apply to the water that a dinosaur drank and the water you drink?

The forked tongue of a snake looks like a stinger as it flickers in and out of its mouth. Is the tongue of a snake actually a stinger?

SURPRISING SCIENCE

An Olympic long-jumper can jump about five times his height— about 30 feet. Good, but not even close to the animal world's champion! What animal is the jumping champion?

Your bones are extremely strong and at the same time, very light. Because they are light, you can move easily and quickly when you need to be speedy. How much do an adult's bones weigh?

SURPRISING SCIENCE

All living things are kept alive by chemical reactions within them. Some reactions are more important than others to all life. What is the most important chemical reaction to all life?

If you like things to be big, you might enjoy growing a monster flower! Rafflesia is a flower that grows and blooms in Malaya and Borneo. How big is Rafflesia?

Many diseases are caused by bacteria. However, they are not all bad and can be quite helpful. For example, many foods are made using bacteria. Name two foods made using bacteria.

DAILY SPECIALS
☆ BAKED BACTERIA
with BACTERIA SOUP
and BACTERIA ALA MODE

Clay soil has very tiny particles. These particles are only a little denser than water. When clay is mixed into water, it is called a colloidal state. What does this colloidal state look like?

The space shuttle requires huge amounts of energy to overcome the Earth's gravity and go into orbit. Going to the moon requires even more energy. Knowing this, can astronauts ever go to Mars?

You have more than 600 muscles in your body. Some muscles are in use all the time, but you may not be aware of them. What do these muscles do?

Water on Earth exists in three phases—solid, liquid, and gas. Solid and liquid water are unusual because the solid is less dense than the liquid. How could you prove this?

Heat is energy. If you heat a cup of water, its particles will move faster than those in a cup of ice water. What happens to particles in melting ice?

The largest part of most soils is pieces of broken rock. Many rocks are broken up when water seeps into cracks and freezes. How does freezing water break up rocks?

The joints that allow the body to move are the result of combinations of bone and muscle. How many joints does a baseball pitcher use to throw a curve ball?

One phase of matter has a definite volume but an indefinite shape. It takes the shape of its container. What phase of matter is this?

The largest frog in the world is named Rana Goliath. It is found in the Congo region of Africa. How big is this giant frog?

There are many harmful bacteria. They produce chemicals called toxins that can poison you. But you can protect yourself. How can you prevent bacteria from harming you?

ANTI-
BACTERIA
SHIELD

A waterfall is a very exciting thing to see. The power of falling water is so great that it can often be harnessed to do work. How is water power used by people?

To live a healthy life, you must supply your body with three basic types of nutrients plus vitamins and minerals. What are the three basic nutrients in your food?

For many animals, a tail is an important part of their bodies. How are tails useful to animals?

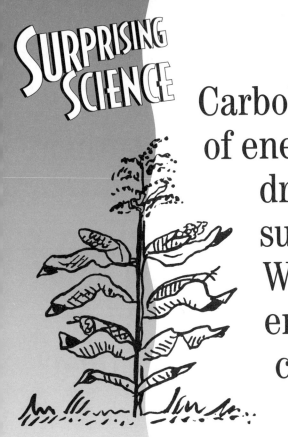

Carbohydrates are a prime source of energy for the body. Carbohydrates, such as starches and sugars, come from plants. Where did the plants get the energy they stored in the carbohydrates?

Connective tissues connect organs and other tissues together. The tissues that connect bones and muscles are called by different names. What are these tissues called?

CONNECTIVE TISSUES

?

?

SURPRISING SCIENCE

Of the three phases of matter, one has neither a definite shape nor a definite volume. Which phase of matter fits this description?

Potential energy comes from the position or condition of an object. Kinetic energy comes from an object's motion. How could you show two kinds of energy in a croquet ball?

The daily cycle of day and night can cause rocks to expand and contract. This can cause rocks to flake. Would you expect more weathering on a north or south slope? Why?

The oldest plants on Earth are about 4,600 years old. These are the bristlecone pines found in the Rocky Mountains. How old are the oldest animals?

When burned, carbon and sulfur form oxides. These oxides can combine with water and form acids. This happens often in clouds. What do we call what falls from these clouds?

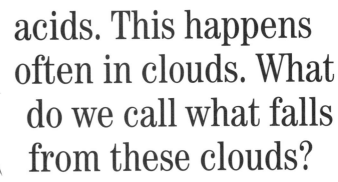

Work is defined as moving a force through a distance. Juan and his backpack weigh 200 pounds. Katie and her backpack weigh 100 pounds. If Juan walks 500 feet and Katie walks 1,000 feet, who did the most work?

Most insects live for one year. They develop over the winter, emerge as adults in the spring or summer, mate, lay eggs, and die. What insect has the longest life span?

Many "new" human developments do what nature has done for thousands of years. For example, sonar can be used to determine what is deep under the sea. Name two animals that use sonar.

SURPRISING SCIENCE

One phase of matter has a definite shape and volume. The book you are reading is this phase of matter. What is the name of this phase of matter?

The rocks that make up the Earth are both useful and beautiful. Often, rocks such as granite, which is very hard and durable, are used in buildings. What is used to cut rock into building blocks?

The green mold you find on old bread is a fungus. This fungus gives off a substance that keeps bacteria from growing near it. It is used as a medicine. What is the name of this medicine?

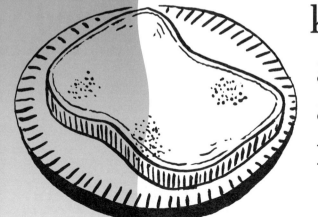

Rivers and streams flow into lakes or oceans. What force causes the movement of the water in streams and rivers?

SURPRISING SCIENCE

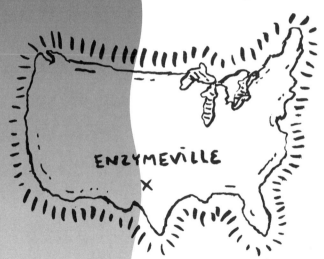

ENZYMEVILLE
X

Enzymes inside your body help digest food. They break the food molecules into smaller pieces that can be used by the body. Where do enzymes come from?

The human skeleton is composed of over 200 bones. Some are moveable, some are not. What are the two main functions of the skeleton?

SURPRISING SCIENCE

If you love pizza, you've got to love fungi. One fungus goes into every pizza and another is a favorite topping. Name the two fungi associated with pizza.

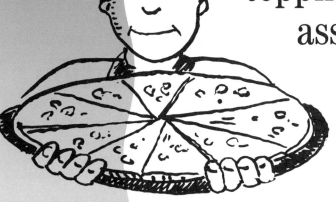

SURPRISING SCIENCE

Animals communicate in many ways. We use speech and other messages. Some animals communicate with smell. How do bees communicate the location of food plants?

SURPRISING SCIENCE

In spring and summer, your porch light attracts moths. Some are quite large. But they are tiny compared to the world's largest moth. How big is the largest moth?

Underground water can dissolve certain kinds of rocks. When this happens underground, caves and caverns are formed. What is the largest cave on Earth?

SURPRISING SCIENCE

The Grand Canyon is the greatest example of weathering on earth. In some places it is about a mile deep. What caused this huge cut in the Earth's surface?

SURPRISING SCIENCE

Fast-moving water can carry soil many hundreds of miles down a river. What happens when the water slows down, such as when it enters an ocean or lake?

One of the most important cycles is the water cycle. During this cycle, water evaporates into the air and returns as rain. This requires energy. Where does this energy come from?

When an idea or observation is not very thorough, we say it is only "skin deep." How deep is the human skin?

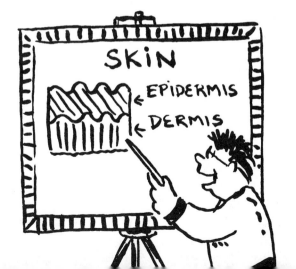

SKIN

← EPIDERMIS

← DERMIS

SURPRISING SCIENCE

Plants come from seeds of all sizes and shapes. What is the world's largest seed and where does it come from?

SURPRISING SCIENCE

When a mass of dense, cold air moves into an area of warm air, the warm air rides up onto the cold. This is called a cold front. Large puffy clouds often mark a cold front. What often happens under a cold front?

The roots of some plants are very different from others. For example, a carrot is a root that supports a plant above. However, a carrot root also serves another function. What is it?

The lowest dry land on Earth is the shoreline of the Dead Sea. It is almost 1,300 feet below sea level. How do you know that the Dead Sea is not connected to the ocean?

If you go to a pond, you will probably see insects running across the surface of the water. If you tried this, you would immediately sink. How can insects walk on water?

You have several different kinds of teeth. Your front teeth are sharp like chisels and can cut and tear tough food. Your back teeth are flat and broad for grinding food. What can you tell about an animal from its teeth?

SURPRISING SCIENCE

Our immune system works constantly to keep us healthy. An important part of the immune system is the body's largest organ. What is the body's largest organ?

There are two types of energy and each can be changed into the other. Kinetic energy is what moving objects have—you can feel it when you catch a ball. What is the other type of energy?

SURPRISING SCIENCE

If you dive into a pool, the pressure gets greater the deeper you go. Submarines that dive deep have to be built of very strong materials. Why aren't deep sea animals crushed?

Primates have well-developed hands and feet that can grab things. In fact some South American primates have a fifth appendage that also can grasp. What is their fifth appendage?

Foods containing large amounts of carbohydrates give quick energy. If you eat a candy bar and get warm, where did that heat energy originally come from?

Covered by mountains and canyons, the Earth is a rugged place. Everyone knows that Mt. Everest is the highest spot. Where is the lowest spot on Earth?

You may think it was cold last winter. However, there are places like Siberia where the temperature can be 50° degrees below zero for weeks. Where is the coldest spot on earth?

Each one of us lives under a pile of air that is miles deep. This stack of air exerts pressure downward on us. What instrument is used to measure air pressure?

Rain often cools things down. However, during or after a rain, the temperature of the air sometimes goes up. Explain how this can happen.

Mammals can keep warm in a wide range of temperatures. Some animals, such as fish and amphibians, are the same temperature as the environment. What happens to amphibians when it gets too cold?

The largest bird eggs come from the ostrich. They can be up to eight inches long and weigh four pounds. Ostrich eggs have been used as water jugs. What is the smallest bird egg? How small is it?

Atoms are made of electrons, protons, and neutrons. Electrons surround a dense nucleus made up of protons and neutrons. What makes up the largest part of the atom?

SURPRISING SCIENCE

Almost all life is dependent on photosynthesis. It combines water and carbon dioxide into carbohydrates that feed living things. What other essential chemical is created by photosynthesis?

When two substances react chemically, a new substance is produced. When iron reacts with oxygen what substance is formed?

OXYGEN + IRON = ?

CHEMICAL CHANGE

If you throw a rock into a lake, it sinks. But you will find that the rock weighs less underwater than on land. What happens when the water around an object has a force greater than the object's weight?

Most animals have either lungs to breathe air or gills to breathe underwater. But a few species have gills at birth and lungs later on. What animals have gills and then lungs?

SURPRISING SCIENCE

The outer layer of your skin is constantly renewed. Millions of cells die and flake off daily. How does the renewal of your skin help protect you against disease?

Wind blows when there are areas of high and low pressure in the atmosphere. Air flows from the area of high pressure to the area of low pressure. Where is the windiest place on Earth?

The deeper you go underwater, the greater the pressure. Pressure is produced by the water above. What is the difference in pressure at three feet underwater compared to one foot underwater?

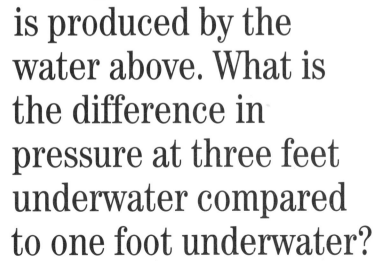

The Earth moves in an elliptical orbit around the sun. There are times when the Earth is closer to the sun than at other times. Is the Earth's distance from the sun the cause of the seasons?

EARTH

SUN

Plants respond to stimuli such as gravity, water, and light. These responses are called tropisms. A plant's response to gravity is called geotropism. What would a plant's response to light be?

The moon circles the Earth about once a month. Other planets also have moons. Which planet has the most moons?

Animals that live in water can reach enormous sizes because the buoyant force of water supports them. What is the largest fish in the world?

Sharks are a primitive type of fish. While sharks have skeletons, they do not have bones. What material makes up the skeletons of sharks?

SURPRISING SCIENCE

Relative humidity compares the amount of water vapor in the air with the amount it could hold. It changes with temperature. If the relative humidity is 100%, what's the weather like?

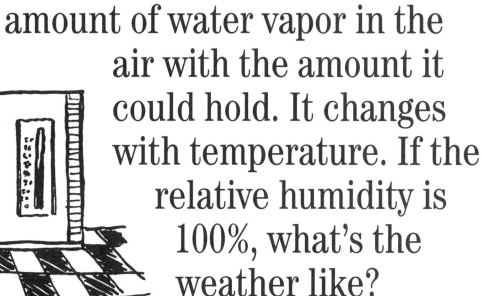

HYGROMETER

"IDENTIFYING AN OBJECT'S PHYSICAL PROPERTIES"

You recognize things by the way they look. A scientists calls this "identifying an object's physical properties." Name some physical properties.

SURPRISING SCIENCE

There are many dangerous animals in the world. Sharks attack humans, as do poisonous snakes. However, these attacks are rare. What is the most dangerous animal?

WORLD'S MOST DANGEROUS #1 CRITTER

?

Circus performers walk on narrow wires high above the crowd. Some even perform tricks on the wire. Which organ gives us a sense of balance?

SURPRISING SCIENCE

You can locate any part of the world with just two numbers. One is distance from the equator along a north-south line. The other is distance east or west of that line. What are the names of these two numbers?

Every English word is made from the 26 letters in our alphabet. Likewise, every chemical compound is made from just over one hundred basic materials. What are these basic materials called?

PERIODIC CHART OF THE ELEMENTS

Many animals migrate. Canadian caribou travel several hundred miles each year. Geese fly the width of North America spring and fall. What animal has the longest migration?

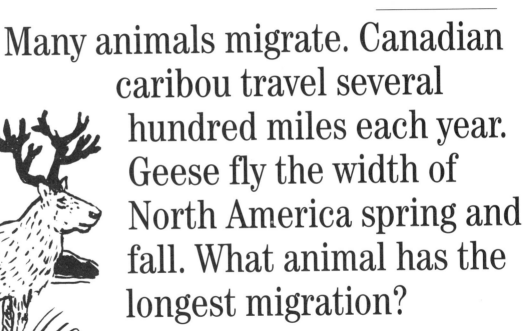

SURPRISING SCIENCE

Mammals can pull heavy weights and run fast. However, for their weight, insects are much stronger and faster. Why are insects stronger and faster?

SALT

One convenient way to classify animals is by whether they have backbones or not. If animals without backbones are called invertebrates, what should animals with backbones be called?

INVERTEBRATE

The larger planets in our solar system are made up of gasses and other light materials. Saturn, a very large planet, is so light that it would float on water. Which planet is the heaviest?

One characteristic of gasses is that they have an indefinite volume. When you squeeze them, they get smaller. If you put twice as much pressure on a gas, what will happen to its volume?

HIGH

MEDIUM

LOW

When it is noon in New York, it is 11 A.M. in Chicago, 10 A.M. in Denver, and 9 A.M. in San Francisco. Why do we have different times in different places?

NAME THE FIVE PRINCIPAL HUMAN SENSES

All of what we know about the world comes from our senses. Humans have five principal senses. What are the principal senses of humans?

The volume of the largest planet in our solar system is larger than all of the other planets combined. What is the name of this giant planet?

the BIGGEST Planet Around

VOLUME
MIN. → MAX

SURPRISING SCIENCE

Hold a sheet of paper by two corners. Now bring the sheet up close to your mouth and blow over the top. What happens?

SURPRISING SCIENCE

Several groups of living things go through stages in their life where they look much different. For example, insects go through four stages—egg, larva, pupa, and adult. Name any butterfly stage you have seen.

Although most sponges you see are made of plastic, natural sponges are living things. Natural sponges live under the sea and are harvested by divers. Are sponges plants or animals?

As the ice melts in a glass of lemonade, the ice and the lemonade are 32°F. When will the lemonade start to get warmer? Why?

Reptiles live all over the world where the climate permits. In North America, they are represented by many snakes, lizards, and even alligators. What is the world's largest reptile?

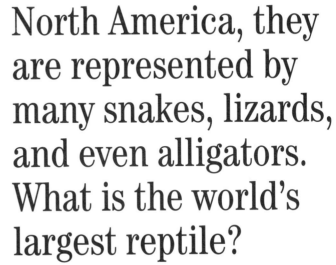

Plasmas are high-energy gasses that conduct electricity and are affected by magnetism. Depending on the gas in them, plasmas emit different colors of light. Where can you see a plasma?

Longitude is measured by the angle between the horizon and an object above the North Pole. This tells you how close you are to the equator. What object in the sky is used to make this measurement?

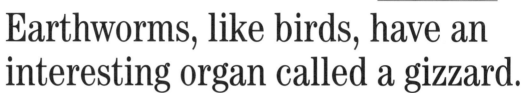

Earthworms, like birds, have an interesting organ called a gizzard. These animals swallow grains of sand and pebbles and store them in their gizzards. What do the sand and pebbles do?

A day and a year are two natural divisions of time you can observe directly. Both of these units are based on the Earth's relationship to another body. What is that other body?

Most seeds can live for several years until conditions are right for growth. Plants use this method to survive cold and drought. How old can a seed be and still grow and blossom?

HOME OF RIP VAN SEED

SURPRISING SCIENCE

1: An insect captured by a spider web

2: The white layer is the oldest.
   Because the layers were laid down one on top of another, the lowest layer (white) must have been laid down before the others and is the oldest.

3: They are both made of cells.

4: Red, Orange, Yellow, Green, Blue, Indigo, and Violet

5: About two-and-one-half times. The Earth is about 25,000 miles in circumference.

6: As one cent is one one-hundredth of a dollar, a centimeter is one one-hundredth of a meter.

7: Have baby cats (kittens). This illustrates the biological principle of "Like comes from like."

8: A ball-and-socket joint that allows your leg to move in many directions. Most hinge joints allow movement in only one direction.

9: Water (H_2O). He took an ice cube from the refrigerator (solid), let it melt (liquid), and then boiled it on the stove turning it into steam (gas).

10: There is another, stronger, force holding you to the surface—gravity.

11: Igneous rock comes from deep in the Earth and is formed under enormous heat and pressure. Igneous rocks underlay all of the continents and make up many islands such as the Hawaiian chain.

12: A bad hare day

13: Ten pints times 1,000 equals 10,000 pints. One gallon equals eight pints. Therefore, 10,000 pints÷8 pints to a gallon equals 1,250 gallons.

14: A decimeter. The prefix *deci-* indicates one-tenth.

15: Most veins have one-way valves that prevent the blood from flowing backward. If these valves were not present, you might faint every time you stood up quickly because the blood would rush from your head.

16: Cells

17: Sedimentary rocks. Rocks such as limestone and sandstone can indicate that the area where they are found was once underwater.

18: The kilogram. Many people are confused by the fact that this is the only basic unit that has a prefix. This causes them to assume that the basic unit is the gram.

19: Friction or lack thereof—in the summer the soles of your shoes create a great deal of friction with the sidewalk. In the winter, if the sidewalk is covered with snow or ice, the surface is very smooth and the shoes create little friction with the surface.

20: Tissues

21: Organs

22: The inertia is caused by mass. Inertia is resistance to changes in motion. Mass resists changes in motion, and the more massive an object, the more it resists being moved.

23: Nancy found fossils. As the sedimentary rocks were laid down, dead fish were covered by layers of sediment. When pressure changed the sediment to rock, the fish's image became part of the rock layer.

24: Neither. They will both hit the ground at about the same time. Gravity accelerates both objects at the same rate. While the bowling ball has a larger force acting on it (its weight), it also has a proportionally larger resistance to movement (inertia).

25: People and animals are consumers. Plants are producers.

26: Plasma

27: Air pressure crushed the bottles. The hot water warmed the bottles and the air in them. When the air cooled and contracted, the pressure in the bottle dropped to less than that of the outside air, and the weak walls of the bottle were pushed in.

28: The shorter days as winter approaches. You might think it would be decreasing temperature, but research has shown it is the decrease in sunlight.

29: The Hawaiian chain is volcanic in origin. Igneous rock originates far below the Earth where no living things exist. In addition, anything buried by eruptions would be consumed by the intense heat

30: before the fossilization process could take place.

As air is accelerated out of the balloon, an equal force in the opposite direction is exerted on the interior of the balloon opposite the opening, causing the balloon to fly around.

31: Asexual reproduction. Common examples of asexual reproduction are budding and runners in plants.

32: That there is a considerable amount of water in the breath you exhale. This water is visible in cold temperatures because it condenses out of air as your warm breath is cooled.

33: The ants. They can lift up to 50 times their own weight. To be equally strong, an Olympic weight lifter would have to lift three large automobiles at once.

34: 120,000. Redheads tend to have fewer, as few as 90,000, and brunettes, being the largest group, are closest to the average.

35: They were all tall. If you cross these tall plants with each other, the recessive trait (short plants) will show up again, but in only one out of four offspring.

36: Neither. They both hit at the same time illustrating that gravity accelerates every object equally. On Earth, air resistance would slow down the feather. However, there is no air on the moon and both objects reacted to gravity alone.

37: Trilobites. Look at the name—Tri (three)–lobe–ite.

38: An optical Aleutian

39: Friction between the soil particles kept them in place. When rain soaked in and lubricated the particles, gravity forced them to move downhill. Another factor is the roots of plants, which also stabilize hillsides. However, when a developer clears the land to build houses, this often kills all the plants and destabilizes the hillside.

40: Yes. The heavy end with the eraser can be balanced by a longer section of the pencil. The short section with the eraser weighs the same as the long section without the eraser. When balanced, your finger is at the point where the weights on either side are equal. This point is called the pencil's center of gravity.

41: Viruses. Viruses are not cells as they do not contain any of the structures of cells and cannot live on their own.

42: The same molecules of water you drink today could very well have been drunk by a dinosaur millions of years ago. The water on Earth today is the same water that was here long ago; it gets recycled over and over again.

43: The flea. An ordinary flea can jump about 200 times the length of its body. To equal this, a human would have to jump approximately 1,200 feet—over one-fifth of a mile!

44: Photosynthesis. Without photosynthesis providing energy to both plants and animals, almost all life would cease.

45: Cheese, yogurt, sauerkraut, and sour cream are just four examples. The holes in Swiss cheese are caused by carbon dioxide given off by bacteria as they covert milk solids into cheese.

46: Going to Mars won't require that much more energy. Correctly aimed and accelerated, a Mars mission will "coast" most of the way through the vacuum of space. The two crucial factors are time (many months) and fuel for the return trip.

47: Float an ice cube in a glass of water. This property is very important. If ice were more dense, lakes would freeze from the bottom and kill everything in them.

48: Water expands when it freezes. If the ice is confined, as in a crack in a rock, it exerts tremendous pressure outward. This pressure, along with daily heating and cooling during the hotter seasons, eventually weathers most exposed rock.

49: A liquid. That a liquid has a definite volume can be demonstrated if you try to compress it. However, the fact that liquids flow shows their indefinite shape.

50: You can prevent them from entering your body by practicing good hygiene; killing bacteria in food by cooking; slowing their growth with refrigeration; and killing them outright with antiseptics.

51: Proteins, carbohydrates, and fats. Typically, proteins are the building blocks of new tissue; fats and carbohydrates supply energy.

52: From the sun. The process of photosynthesis binds the energy from sunlight in the carbohydrates.

53: A gas. Gasses expand out and fill any container they are in. They also take the shape of the container.

54: The south slope. This slope would receive more direct sunlight and experience greater temperature extremes. Thus, it probably would weather more.

55: Acid rain. Too much acid rain can change the chemistry of lakes, damage plants, and erode buildings and rocks.

56: The 17-year locust (periodic cicada). It lives for 17 years, most of it underground as a nymph.

57: It is a solid. Solids may also have other characteristics such as density, color, luster, and hardness.

58: Penicillin. It is made by penicillium fungi and was one of the first of a whole new class of medicines called antibiotics.

59: They are secreted by organs in the digestive system. Some examples are amalase from the salivary glands and pepsin from the stomach.

60: Yeast is used to produce the dough for the crust, and mushrooms are a popular topping.

61: There are moths that live in India and South America that have wingspreads of up to 12 inches.

62: Flowing water, presently represented by the Colorado River. For millions of years, water has flowed down this valley slowly cutting the canyon ever deeper.

63: The sun

64: It is the seed of the double coconut palm tree from Africa. Some can weigh up to 40 pounds, and they take 6 years to ripen.

65: Like other root crops, such as potatoes and beets, a carrot stores food in its root.

66: The attraction of water molecules for each other causes a film on the surface (called surface tension). The insects are light enough so that their feet do not break the film and they can walk on it.

67: The skin. The skin is our first line of defense. As long as it is unbroken, many disease organisms can't affect us.

68: The pressure inside their bodies is the same as that outside. Thus, the effect of the pressure is zero. If you were to raise them to the surface rapidly, they would explode!

69: The sun. Carbohydrates are made by plants through photosynthesis. Photosynthesis stores the energy of sunlight in the carbohydrates when they are made.

70: Antarctica. Recorded temperatures in Antarctica have exceeded -100°F for weeks at a time. The coldest recorded temperature was -126.9°F at the Russian Vostok station in Antarctica.

71: It took energy, usually sunlight, to evaporate the water into the air. When the water condenses and falls as liquid rain, it releases the extra energy it had as a gas. This energy can raise the temperature of the air.

72: Hummingbird eggs are the smallest; they are about the size of a pea.

73: Oxygen. Oxygen is released into the air as a by-product of photosynthesis.

74: It floats. The amount of buoyant force is equal to the weight of the water displaced by the object.

75: Many diseases are caused by bacteria that penetrate the skin. When the skin cells are sloughed off, the bacteria on the surface go with them.

76: It is three times as great. This pressure is exerted in all directions, not just down.

77: Phototropism. "Photo" indicates light as in the name *photosynthesis,* a chemical reaction that requires light.

78: The whale shark. They can be up to 50 feet long and weigh up to 18 tons. Remember that the blue whale, the largest animal that has ever lived, is not a fish but a mammal.

79: If the temperature is above freezing, it is probably raining.

80: The mosquito. Mosquitoes carry many diseases and have been responsible for the death of more people than all of the wars in history.

81: Longitude and latitude. Every point on earth can be represented by just two numbers. Longitude represents how far north or south of the equator you are. Latitude represents how far you are laterally, east or west, from the prime meridian in Greenwich, England.

82: The arctic tern. This bird migrates each year from the Arctic to the southern tip of South America and Africa—14,000 miles!

83: Vertebrates. Remember that the bones that make up the backbone are called vertebrae.

84: It will be squeezed to one-half of its original volume. This is a basic scientific law called Boyle's Law.

85: Sight, touch, smell, taste, and hearing

86: The loose end of the sheet moves up. This happens because moving air exerts less pressure than the still air beneath the sheet. It is an illustration of Bernoulli's principle and explains how an airplane's wing produces lift.

87: They are invertebrate animals.

88: The salt-water crocodile. One specimen from India measured about 33 feet long and weighed about 2 tons.

89: The North Star

90: The sun. A day is the interval that it takes for a point on the Earth's surface to rotate from directly under the sun around to the same point again. A year is the amount of time it takes for the Earth to complete one orbit around the sun.

91: The oldest viable seeds known were from a 2,000-year-old peat bog near Tokyo. They were from a lotus plant and, when planted, sprouted and blossomed.

92: They help grind food. Birds and earthworms do not have teeth and the sand and pebbles are used by the muscular gizzard to grind up their food.

93: Neon signs glow because of the plasma within them. Not all "neon" signs contain neon. Different gasses are used to get different colors. (This is not the same thing as blood plasma, which is a liquid.)

94: The lemonade will get warmer after all of the ice has melted. Until the ice is melted, any extra energy in the drink will melt the ice and the temperature will not change. The energy required to change the phase of a material without changing temperature is called its latent heat.

95: A caterpillar, for example

96: Jupiter. With a diameter of over 86,000 miles, Jupiter is bigger than all of the other planets combined.

97: Because we base local time on the position of the sun in the sky. Noon is when the sun is directly overhead. When the sun is overhead in New York, it is low in the east in San Francisco. San Francisco is three hours "behind" New York because noon arrives in San Francisco three hours later.

98: The Earth. The Earth has an average density of about 5.5 times that of water.

99: Their skeleton is on the outside and covers their bodies. This exoskeleton gives their muscles better leverage and, pound for pound, they are much stronger.

100: Elements. An element is a substance that cannot be broken down further by ordinary chemical means.

101: The ear. In addition to the sense of hearing, the ear contains a series of fluid-filled canals that give us a sense of balance.

102: Color, density, taste, odor, hardness, melting point, boiling point, whether it conducts electricity or heat, whether it is magnetic or not, and, for some compounds, the shape of its crystal

103: Cartilage. Bony fishes developed much later in history.

104: Jupiter, with 12

105: No. The Earth is tilted to the sun, and it is the angle at which the light hits the Earth that determines how much energy is received. This is what determines the seasons. In winter the Earth is tilted away, in summer the light hits it almost directly. The equator, which receives direct sunlight all year long, is the hottest region of the Earth. The Earth is actually closer to the sun in winter!

106: With almost constant gusts, some up to 200 miles per hour, Antarctica is the windiest spot on earth. The fastest recorded winds, over 230 mph, were on Mt. Washington in New Hampshire.

107: Amphibians. Common examples are tadpoles and adult frogs.

108: Rust (iron oxide). Rust has properties that are very different than the iron and oxygen that combined in making it.

109: Empty space. Even compared to the tiny atom, electrons, protons, and neutrons are even smaller.

110: They move, die, or go into a deep resting stage. Some amphibians hibernate, buried in the mud, and only emerge when it warms up. These animals are called cold-blooded, or ectothermic, organisms.

111: A barometer. A barometer is sometimes called a weather gauge because changing air pressure is a key to predicting weather.

112: The Mariana Trench, which is 35,800 feet under the Pacific Ocean near Guam. This is over a mile deeper than Mt. Everest is high.

113: Their tail. New World monkeys have a prehensile tail that can strongly grip things like tree branches. This leaves their four hands and feet free.

114: Potential energy. Potential energy is what a fuel has before it is burned. Most of the time, one type of energy can be converted into the other.

115: What it eats and, to a certain extent, how it lives. An animal that lives by hunting will have sharp and pointed teeth. These will help it catch and eat prey. A cow, on the other hand, has mostly broad, flat teeth that help it grind up the grass and other plants it eats. Human teeth indicate that we eat a broad variety of foods.

116: It is below sea level.

117: Stormy weather— thunderstorms in warm weather and snow flurries in cold. If it is a warm front that is moving, it also rides up on the cold but produces overcast weather and long-lasting rain or snow.

118: At its deepest point, the skin is only about 3/16 of an inch deep.

119: The soil falls out and a delta is formed. One of the best examples of this is where the Mississippi River flows out into the Gulf of Mexico.

120: The largest known single cave is the Big Room in Carlsbad, New Mexico. It is over 4,000 feet long, over 300 feet high, and over 650 feet wide. However, the largest known cave system, over 150 miles long, is Mammoth Cave, Kentucky.

121: With a dance. The bee waggles in a figure-8 dance with a straight portion across the center. The straight portion indicates the direction while the number of figure-8 patterns indicates the distance.

122: Support and protection. The skeleton is the frame upon which the body is constructed. Linked together with ligaments, the larger bones are as strong as metal girders. Some bones, such as those in the skull, are fused together and provide protection for organs such as the brain.

123: Gravity. Lakes and oceans are always lower than the rivers and streams.

124: Harder rocks such as diamonds. Special saws with diamond teeth are used to cut granite into building blocks.

125: Bats, whales, and porpoises all use sonar. We know the most about bats. Their sonar is much more sophisticated than the machines that humans build. Bats can not only determine shapes but also the fine details of targets.

126: They both did exactly the same amount of work—100,000 foot-pounds of work.

127: The oldest animals are probably turtles. Box turtles have been known to live for as long as 100 years. The larger turtles may live for 200 years.

128: A croquet ball on a sloping lawn has potential energy. If you hit it, it has kinetic energy.

129: Ligaments and tendons are tissues that connect muscles and bones.

130: Monkeys and opossums use their prehensile tails as an extra "hand" and for balance. Cows and horses use tails as fly swatters. Fish use tails as rudders in swimming. A beaver uses its flat tail to swim and to slap the water and warn of danger. Lizards can shed their tails to escape predators.

131: Falling water was once used to turn waterwheels and run all kinds of machinery that ground flour, sawed lumber, and ran looms to weave fabrics. Today falling water is used to power huge turbines that produce electricity.

132: Rana Goliath is 1 foot long. Imagine what it might sound like when it croaks!

133: Counting all the joints in his fingers, a pitcher will use 17 different joints in his arm and hand in pitching any ball. But there are also joints in his legs and feet that are used too.

134: The particles on the surface of the ice move faster than those within the ice. They collide with the slower moving particles and give them energy. The slower moving ice particles move faster. As they move faster, they move further apart, which we can observe as melting.

135: Heart muscles pump blood through your body. Stomach muscles help digest foods. Diaphragm muscles help you breathe. Tiny muscles in your ears help you hear!

136: It will look muddy! Because the particles of clay are so tiny and only a little denser than water, it will take a long time for the clay to settle out.

137: Rafflesia measures up to three feet across. It is brown and purple and parasitic on other plants. If you wanted to grow it, your neighbors would probably object because it has a scent like rotting meat!

138: In a 160-pound man, the bones will weigh only 29 pounds.

139: No. A snake's tongue is more like a feeler. Snakes use their tongues to touch. They may use their tongues to help them smell.

140: It protects against harmful sunlight and bacteria, controls your body temperature, and keeps the body from drying out. The skin also picks up messages from your environment. Nerves in the skin relay messages to the brain.

141: The temperature of the cookie is higher than the milk because the kinetic energy of the cookie particles is higher than the kinetic energy of the cold milk. A useful analogy is to think of a thermometer as a molecular speedometer.

142: Increases in the volume and velocity of water. The standing water damages homes and crops. The fast-flowing stream carries away soil, rocks, and boulders, and erodes the banks.

143: Bones grow and change as we grow older. Certain structures are shaped differently in men and women. Broken bones and bones that have been stressed by disease are distinguishable from healthy bones.

144: On April 12, 1934, the weather station on top of Mount Washington recorded a blast that measured 231 miles per hour!

145: Ostriches cannot fly, but they can run at speeds of about forty miles an hour. They can also deliver ferocious kicks!

146: Protein is used to make parts of every cell in your body. Even your bones are made up of protein plus compounds of calcium and phosphorus.

147: The heat from the sidewalk comes from the sun. The sidewalk can actually store some heat and on a very hot day will feel quite warm hours after sundown.

148: Some glaciers still exist in Alaska, Iceland, and Switzerland. Geologists have studied their effect on the land around them. Glaciers leave scratches and gouges on rocks as they move. They also pile up debris in hills called moraines. Moraines are found in places where there are no glaciers today. Rocks that bear the marks of glaciers are also found near moraines.

149: Both the football player and the pitcher depend on joints called ball-and-socket joints. The pelvis and the shoulder are both examples of the ball-and-socket joint. Hinge joints are also involved, but the special motions required to do these two special things involve ball-and-socket joints.

150: The clam called Tridacna gigas can be up to 43 inches long and 29 inches wide, and it can weigh as much as 579 pounds.

151: Probably the gray parrot. Gray parrots have been taught to count, to learn colors, and to say many words. Unlike other parrots, they seem to know the meaning of words—and use them properly.

152: When you get too warm, you perspire. As the moisture on your skin evaporates, you feel cooler. This is because heat that evaporates the sweat is drawn from the skin. When you are cold, you get "goosebumps"—your skin's effort to minimize heat loss.

153: Large lakes provide a source of moisture and stabilize temperatures. Prevailing winds passing over the water pick up moisture and release it over the shoreline. Since water cools less quickly than air, lakes also tend to prevent sharp temperature changes on land nearby.

154: The Colorado Rockies may not receive as much snow as the Swiss Alps do and most of it melts. Much of the moisture that comes from the Pacific Ocean is lost to the mountains of the West Coast.

155: People have grown wheat for over 10,000 years. It is still one of the most common grains throughout the world.

156: Ducks' feathers are waterproof because of the oil that covers them. An oil gland near the duck's tail supplies oil. Ducks pick up some of the oil in their bills and spread it over their feathers. If you have ever seen a duck preening its feathers, this is what it was doing.

157: Mistletoe is green. This indicates that some form of photosynthesis occurs in the plant's leaves. However, mistletoe requires a host plant to supply minerals and water.

158: Carbohydrates are foods that supply energy that can be released quickly. There are three kinds of carbohydrates—sugar, starches, and fiber. Fruits such as apples and pears contain high amounts of sugar. Bread and pastas contain starch. Peas and beans have large amounts of fiber.

159: It is friction, produced by mechanical energy. This same kind of energy can produce enough heat to start a fire when two pieces of wood are rubbed together.

160: Both the hamburger and the French fries are high in fat. Hamburgers have a lot of saturated fat (fat that comes from animal products). French fries are cooked in oil, an unsaturated fat (which comes from plants), which they tend to absorb. Fats should make up less than 30 percent of your diet for good health.

161: Water and temperature changes cause the forces that break up rocks.

162: Meteors leave craters on the Earth's surface. The largest meteor crater is the Vredevort Ring in South Africa. It measures 26 miles across and may be half a billion years old.

163: It's hard to believe, but there are 29 bones in your skull! Anthropologists can tell a person's age by examining the bones of the skull. In adults, these bones are fused.

164: Bats use echolocation (SONAR) to find their way. They make high-pitched squeaks that create sound waves. The sound waves bounce off any nearby object. Bats hear the sound waves as echoes and can steer clear of objects and each other!

165: The pigment is anthocyanin. Its colors can range all the way from pale pink to deep purple.

166: The heat is penetrating Rondell's ankle by direct contact. When heat energy moves directly from a source to an object, it is called conduction.

167: The human body is 60%–75% water. This means that your cells are mostly water. Your blood is mostly water and it carries other nutrients to all parts of your body. Water helps get rid of waste materials. Water, given off through sweat, helps to cool your body. You also loose water in your breath.

168: No, the Grand Canyon was formed by water cutting through rock. Some of this water may have come from Ice Age glaciers but most did not. It has taken millions of years to form the canyon.

169: It's surprising to know that even though winter temperatures reach –60°F, yellow poppies will grow and bloom in the Arctic summers.

170: The spine enables humans to stand upright. It supports the ribs and the skull and acts as a conduit for the nervous system.

171: Yes, cows, goats, sheep, deer, and camels all chew cuds. These animals belong to a group called ruminants. Ruminants have specials stomachs that break down foods that are hard to digest.

172: Cold air is denser than warm air. This is the reason that warm air rises. But as warm air rises, it gives off some of its heat, becomes cooler, and starts to sink. This process causes convection currents. If you have ever seen hawks or sailplanes (gliders) climbing, it is these convection currents (called thermals) that are carrying them higher.

173: It was probably carried there by a glacier during the Ice Age. These boulders are called erratics and are quite common in areas that show other signs of glaciation, such as moraines.

174: When your chest cavity gets bigger it causes reduced air pressure in the cavity. Outside air, under a higher pressure, flows into your lungs. When your diaphragm relaxes, the opposite happens.

175: The same way that light gets here—as radiation. Electromagnetic waves carrying energy in many different forms travel through space at the speed of light.

176: No. What she is seeing is the property of most substances to expand when they are warm and contract when cold.

177: Sedimentary rock. Sandstone is a good example of the end product of this process. Limestone is also a sedimentary rock, but it is usually produced by chemical action.

178: Almost all of it is given off as waste heat. For example, most of the energy given off by a light bulb is heat, the energy of a car is converted to heat by its brakes as it slows down, and the heat from your furnace eventually leaks into the outside environment.

179: The first cameras used strips of copper called plates. These plates were covered with a chemical that changed when light touched it. Developing the chemical made the picture appear.

180: When sunlight passes through the glass jar and the water, it is bent (refracted). Each color in the light bends a little differently. Violet bends most and red bends least.